WHERE'S THE PIZZA BOY?
A Search - and - Find Book

SCHOLASTIC INC.

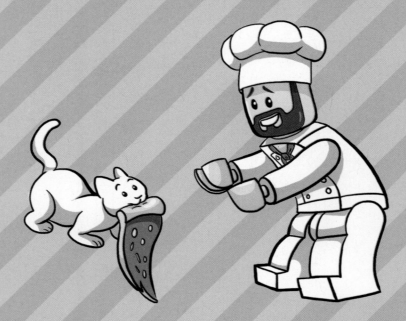

ISBN 978-0-545-60805-3

LEGO, the LEGO logo, the Brick and Knob configurations and Minifigure are trademarks of the LEGO Group. © 2013 The LEGO Group. Produced by Scholastic Inc. under license from the LEGO Group. All rights reserved. Published by Scholastic Inc.

12 11   17 18/0

Printed in the U.S.A.
First printing, June 2013

MAMMA MIA!
This airheaded
PIZZA DELIVERY BOY
has mixed up the orders again.
Help me find him before he
delivers the wrong pizzas to
my customers!

RUSH HOUR!

LEGO® City is a busy place, and at rush hour it's even more crowded! It might be hard to find our pizza delivery boy with so many people around. See if you can find him. Remember—he's the one with the pizza!

You found him already? Good for you. Now try to find this stuff:

- three WANTED posters for a crook
- the crook on the WANTED poster
- three dogs
- two orange motorcycles
- eleven blue skateboards
- a man with ice cream
- a man with a camera
- a blue bowl with cookies
- a firefighter
- two yellow taxis

CITY CLEAN-UP!

Sometimes, LEGO City gets a bit messy—but the local street cleaners work hard to tidy up. While they do their job, see if you can find our delivery boy. Hopefully, he has not delivered the wrong pizza yet!

SPOT THE DIFFERENCE

Did you spot our pizza boy? Fantastic!
It's time for another challenge then.
Look carefully at this picture and try to find
ten tiny differences from the opposite page.

STREET ROCK!

Street concerts are a great place to listen to music. Today, a famous rocker girl is arriving to join a guitar player and play a show. But the whole street is full of excited performers and fans. Can you see our pizza boy hiding in the crowd?

SPOT THE DIFFERENCE

Well done! It wasn't as difficult as it seemed, was it? Now it's time for something a bit more challenging. The picture below has ten small differences from the page opposite. Look carefully and try to spot them.

BEACH TIME!

Some people like to swim in the salty sea. Others enjoy hanging out on the sand and sunbathing. The LEGO City beach always has lots to do. You can drive a boat, go fishing, or if you get hungry, you can order a pizza. Speaking of pizza, where's the pizza boy?

If you have found our pizza delivery boy, try to spot:

- four red bicycles
- three pink crabs
- a pair of green flippers
- a message in a bottle
- a white cat
- a blue inflatable duck with white spots
- a green submarine
- a man with a camera
- gray binoculars
- a boy with a white volleyball

13

HARBOR HIJINKS!

The LEGO City Harbor is bustling with activity and people at work. A ship has arrived with crates of fish, but that's not the only cargo it brought home. Looks like a few surprises await the people at the pier. Can you find the pizza boy among the chaos?

SPOT THE DIFFERENCE

You found him again? You're good at this! Now see if you can find ten differences between these two pictures.

SOCCER CELEBRATION!

The local soccer team won the trophy! The crowds are welcoming the players home at the airport, and everybody wants an autograph or a photo with the winners. Did someone order a pizza? I think I see our pizza delivery boy—do you?

If you already found the pizza boy, try to spot these things:

- nine soccer balls
- a white cat
- a gold trophy
- a girl with a camera
- a man who is spilling milk from his mug
- a surfer
- a handcuffed robber
- a maraca player wearing a sombrero
- a soccer player giving an autograph
- a firefighter

BEAR AT THE AIRPORT?

Traveling by plane is very exciting, but waiting for your flight can be pretty boring—unless you're in LEGO City. Who brought a bear here? And where's that pizza boy?

ARRIVALS		DEPARTURES	
New York City	9:25		
Denver	12:10	New York City	7:50
Los Angeles	5:40	Denver	10:05
Austin	7:15	Los Angeles	11:20
		Austin	1:35

SPOT THE DIFFERENCE

You did it! That's great! Are you ready for the next task? Spot the ten differences between the picture below and the one on the previous page.

ARRIVALS			DEPARTURES	
New York City	9:25			
Denver	12:10		New York City	7:50
Los Angeles	5:40		Denver	10:05
Austin	7:15		Los Angeles	11:20
			Austin	1:35

SPACE LAUNCH!

Everyone wants to see a rocket fly into space! So today, the LEGO City spaceport is packed with people and space fans. There are astronauts, the ground crew, police, and even a . . . mime? But where's that pizza boy?

After you find the pizza delivery boy, try to spot:

- a clown
- a hitchhiker
- a man with binoculars
- a sleeping firefighter
- a man wearing a white towel around his hips
- a boy with a pink lollipop
- a mime artist
- a satellite dish
- a police motorcycle
- two TV cameramen

GOLD RUSH!

The miners have struck gold, and it looks like everyone else wants a piece of the action! Everyone wants to be rich, but who ordered a pizza? The chef is close to catching up with the pizza delivery boy. Can you find both of them?

HB 2846

SECURITY

SPOT THE DIFFERENCE

Brilliant! Not only have you found the pizza boy, but also the chef. Can you also find ten differences between the picture on this page and the one opposite?

FOREST FRENZY!

The city police are visiting the forest rangers for a training session. But it looks like there's been a prison break— at lunchtime! While the police and rangers catch the crooks, see if you can find the pizza boy.

If you have found the pizza delivery boy, try to spot:

- three squirrels
- ten police dogs
- five pairs of handcuffs
- a man with a map
- three police motorcycles
- a crook with a big brown bag
- a crook with a crowbar
- three mushrooms
- two black wrenches
- two policemen wearing white helmets

NATURE PICNIC!

The people who live in LEGO City love to come to nature, especially for the annual spring picnic! Whether they've come to fly a kite, go water-skiing, or play with wildlife, it's a great time for everyone. Except maybe the pizza boy. It looks like the pizza chef finally found him! Did you?

If you have found the pizza delivery boy, try to spot:

- Three envelopes with red stamps
- A teddy bear
- Two cheerleaders
- A skateboarder
- Five black helmets

- A green bicycle
- A diver
- A bear
- Two gray walkie-talkies
- A magnifying glass

FIREFIGHTER FUN!

Firefighters work hard, but even they need a day off. So they've come to the woods to test their skills and relax. Some check their hoses, some barbeque, and others practice catching cows in their rescue nets. Hey! Has the pizza arrived yet? They've been waiting all day. Where's the pizza boy?

If you have found the pizza delivery boy, try to spot:

- twelve cows
- a man with a basket full of mushrooms
- two cameramen
- a man taking a photo nine fish
- a red tie
- a frightened firefighter covering his eyes
- eight firefighter's vehicles
- three firefighters holding axes
- a firefighter with a whistle

ANSWERS:

PAGE 6-7: RUSH HOUR!

PAGE 8-9: CITY CLEAN-UP!

PAGE 10-11: STREET ROCK!

PAGE 12-13: BEACH TIME!

PAGE 14-15: HARBOR HIJINKS!

PAGE 16-17: SOCCER CELEBRATION!

PAGE 18-19: BEAR AT THE AIRPORT?

PAGE 20-21: SPACE LAUNCH!

PAGE 22-23: GOLD RUSH!

PAGE 24-25: FOREST FRENZY!

PAGE 26-27: NATURE PICNIC!

PAGE 28-29: FIREFIGHTER FUN!

BUILD YOUR LEGO® LIBRARY!